AOLÉON

The Martian Girl

PART THREE

**This is Part Three of a five-part series.
Parts one through five are:**

The Martian Girl

PART THREE

Brent LeVasseur

For all media inquiries, publishing, merchandising, or licensing:
aoleon@aoleonthemartiangirl.com

For information regarding permissions, e-mail Aoléon USA at:
aoleon@aoleonthemartiangirl.com
or use the Contact Us page at:
http://aoleonthemartiangirl.com

Visit Aoléon The Martian Girl website for more information at:
http://aoleonthemartiangirl.com.

ISBN Hardcover: 978-0-9791285-6-1
ISBN Paperback: 978-0-9791285-5-4
ISBN eBook: 978-0-9791285-0-9

Published in the U.S.A.

Welcome to Part 3 of a five-part series.

TABLE OF CONTENTS

LUMINON
CHAPTER NINE

LUMINON'S PALACE, MARTIAN MEGALOPOLIS, OLYMPUS MONS, PLANET MARS

In the center of the Martian megalopolis stood a colossal fortress, a citadel — the newly acquired palace for the Luminon after his army had overthrown the democratically elected government, the Supreme Council of Twelve. The enormous palace, constructed as an architectural tribute to the Luminon's power, was designed to trigger a feeling of insignificance to any foreign dignitary who might pay the Luminon a visit. Standing more than two miles high, the palace conveyed the essence of power. Near the top of the citadel resided the Luminon's main throne room with its high-arching ceilings and huge portal windows on every side that presented the Luminon with spectacular views of the entire megalopolis.

In a flash of light, Aoléon and Gilbert phased to the top of the Luminon's palace, having made the jump directly from her home. Gilbert caught his breath as he fought off the shock of phasing and the disorientation that followed. Viewing the layout of the buildings of the megalopolis from high above, Gilbert could see that the pattern they formed resembled quite closely the center of a sunflower. The megalopolis was designed and arranged in concentric overlapping spiral rings based on phi, the golden ratio, giving him the feeling that the city was somehow a giant living organism, and he was a bumblebee perched on top of its center-most bud.

The largest buildings were placed in the outer ring, farthest from the center of the megalopolis and the citadel, with the buildings gradually getting smaller, at the rate of the golden ratio, the closer they were positioned to the center. This architectural feat was designed so that when the Luminon gazed out of his window onto the city below, none of the buildings seemed any larger than the ones in front of it and certainly not larger than his citadel. It was an optical illusion, of course. However, it gave the false impression that none of the buildings were taller than the citadel where Aoléon and Gilbert now stood.

At that moment, though, the view from the top of the citadel was the last thing on Aoléon's and Gilbert's minds.

Instead, they focused their attention on the business at hand — a force-field barrier that protected the opening to an air duct.

"We need to go in through there," Aoléon stated. "But first we have to deactivate the field barrier."

Gilbert reached out a hand to touch the force field.

"Wait!" Aoléon screamed and knocked Gilbert to the ground just before he could touch the force field with his outstretched hand.

"Uhhh…what'd you do that for?!" Gilbert slowly picked himself up.

"That is a fifty terawatt force field. Had you touched it just now, you would have been vaporized. Come on, we need to deactivate the field first using the omnitool Bizwat gave me," Aoléon said as she took a small device out of her pocket that was about the size of a cell phone.

"You're going to use a device the *pizza guy* gave you to try to break into the palace? Are you crazy?"

"No, silly! Bizwat is not just *any* pizza delivery guy — he is part of a super-elite and *covert* Martian commando unit.

He specializes in things like this. Pizza delivery is just his *cover*. The device he gave me should be able to hack through the security system and deactivate the shield around this portal. Without this device, it would be almost impossible to get in."

Gilbert grunted an acknowledgment and stood back as Aoléon approached the portal. She activated the device, aiming it at the suspensor field. Gilbert could hear a sonic pitch rising, the frequency of the force field wavering in and out of flux. Finally, the force field collapsed, and Aoléon slid the device back into her small hip-purse.

"There. The field is deactivated. Now we go in. Follow me," Aoléon directed as she jumped and slid down through the portal opening. Gilbert hesitated for a moment, gathered up his courage, and followed after her. *If she can do it, so can I*, he thought as he leapt downward into the blackness.

"Ooooeeeeee," Aoléon cried as she slid down into the darkness below.

"Oh my God, oh my God…," Gilbert repeated, jumping after her.

They landed several levels below in a main ventilation shaft. From there, it was about a half hour of crawling and floating through tight spaces — some of the tubes contained gravity-displacement paneling that enabled you to float down the tube.

Gilbert found it incredibly difficult to stay relaxed. A sudden wave of claustrophobia swept over him.

He was used to working in wide-open spaces such as his farm in Nebraska where you could see for miles in every direction. Being in a confined space like this ventilation tube was new to him, and his body reacted negatively. Feeling the onset of a panic attack, he began to hyperventilate. He tried as hard as he could to control his breathing while looking straight ahead, but that only helped a little. Aoléon, sensing Gilbert's discomfort, telepathically sent him her γαλήνη (calm/serenity).

"That's better. Thanks!"

As Gilbert crawled down the ventilation tube with Aoléon's help, he contained his fear and suppressed the onrush of claustrophobia. Suddenly, he heard metallic ticks from behind him in the tube. "Aoléon, something is coming

up behind me," Gilbert whispered. A jolt shook him. The tube lit up with blue flashes.

"AAAAH!" Gilbert screamed as he was struck by an electrical-plasma discharge that emanated from the darkness. He kicked out behind him and felt his boot hit something metallic. He then heard it move up the side of the tube closer to his head.

Two glowing red lights illuminating what looked like a mechanical form emerged from the shadows. It recoiled, readying itself to attack him again, so he quickly grabbed it with his gloved hands and found that the bot was relatively light. In the midst of grappling with it, it shocked him again and again with an electrical-plasma discharge.

While struggling to keep hold of it, Gilbert's teeth chattered together from being shocked repeatedly by the bot. "A-a-a-a-o-o-o-o-l-l-l-l-e-e-e-e-u-u-u-u-n-n…h-h-h-h-h-h-h-h-help!" Gilbert cried as he repeatedly slammed the bot into the side of the tube wall until it finally ceased to move. He watched as its glowing eye flickered and then died.

"That was close," Gilbert sighed.

"Are you all right?" whispered Aoléon.

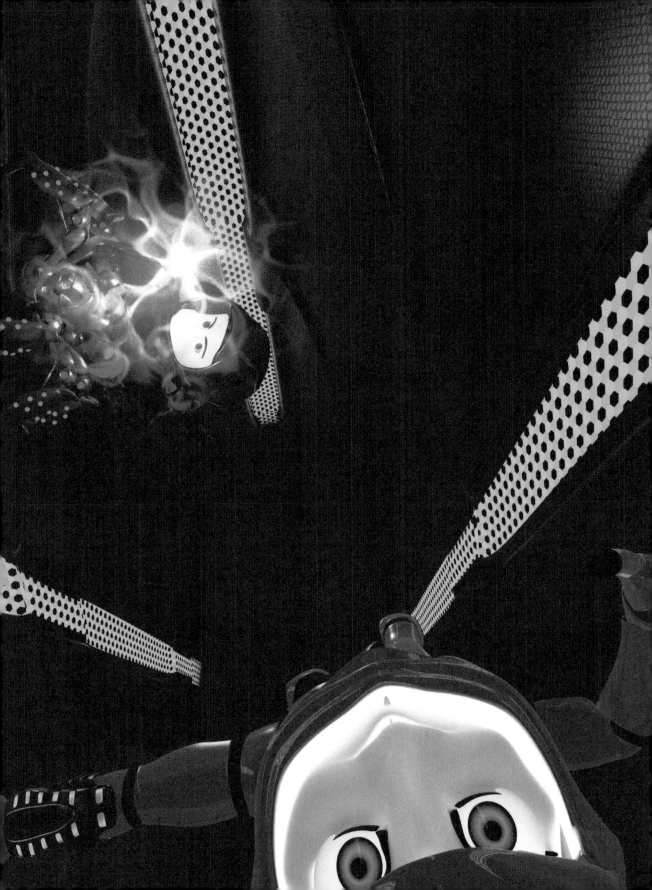

"Yeah, I think so. No permanent damage. Just shocked me a bit and scared the heck out of me is all," Gilbert replied laughing nervously.

"I think that was a maintenance bot. I hope that it did not have time to send a signal to alert security." Aoléon removed the omnitool that Bizwat had lent her from her hip-purse and checked the holographic map to make sure they were heading in the right direction. "Come on, let us keep moving — we are almost there." Aoléon continued down the tube at an accelerated pace.

Eventually, they found their way into the main ventilation tube situated directly above the vestibule leading into the Luminon's throne room. Peering down through a ventilation duct into what appeared to be the throne room proper, Gilbert had no difficulty spotting the Luminon who had strutted into view. Gilbert immediately noticed that the Luminon was unusually tall and muscular, especially for a Martian and even for a human. He wore a tightly fitting body suit that accentuated his unusually large muscles and was trailed by a long flowing cape. He had a chiseled face with cold, piercing eyes that gave Gilbert the chills. The Luminon stood with several of his minions who were half

his size. Gilbert's senses suddenly prickled as he felt what could be described only as the presence of something evil.

They watched intently as two Royal Paladin Elite Guards led a trembling Martian drone out onto the platform before the Luminon. The guards nudged him forward. "Ouch! Ouch! That hurts!" exclaimed the prisoner.

"Where are the rebels hiding?" demanded the Luminon.

"No, no, I do not know. Please! I am loyal to the Luminon — not a dissident!"

"You are lying!" screamed the Luminon as he struck the prisoner with his immense psionic powers, sucking the drone's life force from his body. He struck him again with blasts of energy draining even more life from the now-weakened prisoner. His grey eyes seemed to flash with enjoyment each time he took a little more life from his prisoner.

"Ahhhh…I swear I do not know!" the prisoner screamed.

"If you tell me, I will spare your feeble life."

"A-All right. All right…Many of them work in the Galact-works. They sometimes have their meetings in the Old

Enterprise Clave, but they frequently change locations. There! That is all I know. Now please let me go," the prisoner pleaded.

"Thank you. And now…time to die," the Luminon said coldly with a wave of his arm.

"But…b-but…you s-said you would let me l-live!" The prisoner protested as his knees buckled and his legs bowed like a pair of slinky toys. The guards had to grab him to keep him from falling over completely.

"I lied." The Luminon raised his hands, releasing life-draining psionic energy. The Martian prisoner screamed until the walls muffled his cries as his face hit the floor. The room resounded with the Luminon's laughter. "You are weak, just like the rest of your pathetic species! Dispose of him."

Aoléon and Gilbert exchanged astonished glances, unable to believe what they had just witnessed.

"This is getting tire-sssome," hissed the Luminon. He activated a large holokronic display. "Bring me Cerberus and Sisyphus at once! I want the dissidents found and crushed!" With a swirl of his cape, the Luminon turned away from the holokron and cut the communications link. The projection vanished.

A deep thrumming sounded as the large portal to the throne room opened. Gilbert had to blink several times to make sure he wasn't hallucinating. He watched as two of the strangest-looking Martians he had ever seen entered the throne room. The first appeared to be a hybrid abomination of Martian and machine — a half Martian man and half robot. The Martian's upper torso connected seamlessly to the robot's abdomen like a mechanical centaur. The robotic lower half had four metallic legs and two retractable pincer arms. Each of its legs scraped the floor as it walked into the room.

The second Martian entered the throne room following the Martian/robot hybrid. This Martian, like the Luminon, was unusually tall with a muscular build. He was much taller than any other Martian Gilbert had seen thus far, with the exception of the Luminon himself.

"Presenting Sisyphus, Head of Martian Intelligence and Cerberus, Chief Scientist of the BotWorks," announced the Luminon's Chief of Security. Sisyphus and Cerberus entered the room and bowed in front of the Luminon. (Cerberus's arachnoid exabot front legs dipped, enabling him to fake a bow.)

"I just finished interrogating a rebel spy. He claims the leaders of the rebellion are working in the Galactworks and meeting in the Old Enterprise Clave. Send in the paladin guard to suppress the rebellion," commanded the Luminon.

"My Luminon, there is another alternative you might consider," Sisyphus hesitantly replied. "The Martian people are a peaceful race. They have no taste for war. If we use troops and declare martial law, you will have a full uprising on your hands. He paused. However, if we were to use a more devious means to get the people behind an invasion of Terra…"

"What do you propose?"

"Imagine for a moment if an 'accident' were to occur at the Galactworks that disrupted the flow of galactmilk. People would then begin to starve, which could then be blamed on dissident rebel factions and used to sway the hearts and minds of the people in favor of invading Terra for their precious milk supply."

"They would then view the presence of our troops as a protective rather than suppressive force. Clever," hissed the Luminon. "So clever, in fact, that I am surprised I did not think of it myself. The Martian people are nothing if not a bunch of dumb, useless eaters that will gladly hand over all of their freedoms to feel more secure. In fact, after the galact processing is crippled, they will beg us to intervene! Make it so!" the Luminon commanded. He then motioned for Cerberus to deliver his report.

Cerberus fidgeted inside his arachnoid exabot. When he spoke, his voice squeaked. "My Luminon, the bot army is nearing completion and shall be ready for deployment very soon. I would like to present a formal invitation to the BotWorks for a full demonstration of the new models."

"Excellent! Everything is progressing according to my plan. Very soon Terra and its precious milk supply will fall into Martian hands, and all of Terra will be mine!"

"There is another matter…A Xiocrom sentinel intercepted a communication from Pax. He spoke with a Martian girl named Aoléon and someone else whom we were unable to identify. The Xiocrom believes that the other person may in fact be a Terran boy, but that has yet to be confirmed," reported Sisyphus.

"I want the Martian girl and the hu-mon captured immediately and brought to me for interrogation," the Luminon commanded. He waved his arm, motioning for Sisyphus and Cerberus to leave.

"As you wish, my Luminon." Sisyphus and Cerberus bowed deeply and exited the throne room.

Gilbert, his eyes wide, turned toward Aoléon and whispered frantically. "The Luminon is searching for us!"

"Shhhh, I know," she snapped. "My father works at the Galactworks! I have to warn him."

"Good idea." *In the meantime, I will try not to make a mess in my suit,* he thought to himself. Gilbert's attention returned to the Luminon below them.

"Once we have conquered Terra and acquired its precious milk supply, I shall have absolute power!" raved the Luminon, shaking his fist vigorously. While the Luminon spoke those words, Gilbert watched as the Luminon's face momentarily shifted into another form and then quickly transformed back again. Gilbert glanced at Aoléon, frightened and confused, but she acted as if she saw nothing unusual.

"Did you see that?!"

"What?"

"Just then! The Luminon…he just changed shape!"

"Changed into what?"

"That was weird! But I'm not sure what I saw."

"We need to go now. We need to warn my father!"

"Father?"

"Sisyphus is going to sabotage the Galactworks, and my father manages the pumps!" Aoléon grabbed Gilbert by the wrist, and in a flash they phase-jumped away.

GALACTWORKS
CHAPTER TEN

GALACTWORKS, MARTIAN MEGALOPOLIS, OLYMPUS MONS PLANET MARS

Deep down inside the bowels of the extinct Martian volcano, Olympus Mons, at the lowest point of the Martian megalopolis, stood the Galactworks. The Galactworks produced millions of gallons of galactmilk daily for the Martian people to consume. Deimos, Aoléon's father, managed the pump operations, which were located in an open cavern filled with rows of robotic milk pumps. Each pump was attached to several bovars — the Martian equivalent to Earth's milk cows. The bovars had enormous rear ends, which were surpassed only by the amount of gas they expelled as a result of their incessant eating — something necessary to produce the large quantities of galactmilk that the Martian people relied on daily for their galact food production needs.

The pumps were responsible for sucking the milk from the bovars and processing it into galact. Each of the pumps

was connected to multiple bovars, but Gilbert noticed that many of the pumps were missing bovars and were inactive. Suddenly, he remembered an offhand comment by Deimos when Gilbert first visited Aoléon's home — that many of the bovars mysteriously had gone missing. Each pump was shaped like a wheel, had tubes connected to the central pump mechanism, and most had a Martian drone operator to monitor and control its function.

Aoléon and Gilbert phased into the large cavern.

"This is where all the galact processing takes place," said Aoléon.

"What exactly are we doing here?"

"The Luminon is planning to sabotage the pumps, so keep a lookout for anything unusual."

Anything unusual? thought Gilbert. *It ALL seems pretty darn unusual to me.*

Deus ex machina, I forgot Zoot! Aoléon thought.

"You did?" Gilbert replied, hearing her thoughts.

"Yes. My Martian precognition is telling me we will need him," she said. "Wait here while I fetch him."

Before Gilbert could reply with an "Okay," Aoléon had phase-jumped away. A few seconds later she reappeared with Zoot by her side.

Zoot scampered over to a bovar pump and proceeded to pee on it. Aoléon scowled and gave him a strong telepathic rebuke, which caused Zoot to scamper off. A moment later, Zoot sensed that something was wrong and signaled Aoléon. "BRRREEET!"

"What is wrong boy?" Aoléon inquired, speaking more to herself than to Zoot because all of her communications with him were telepathic.

"What is it?" Gilbert inquired.

"Zoot is sensing something out of the ordinary."

A moment passed, and then Zoot continued on sniffing each bovar pump and climbing over it like a tree frog with his suction-cup hands and feet.

"Guess it was nothing," Aoléon commented, and they continued to walk through the facility.

Unnoticed by the worker drones or the staff, a cloaked Martian quietly entered the pumping room. Silently, the stealthy form planted explosive charges on several of the galact pumps while remaining hidden from the drone operators who sat on top of them. After setting his final charge, the form approached an enormous maintenance bot. Maintenance bots came in dozens of different models and types: they ranged from small to large and did every-thing from taking out the garbage to replacing spent fusion reactor cores. This particular one was enormous, designed specifically to replace damaged galact pumps. The saboteur climbed up the back of the enormous maintenance bot, which was about three stories tall, and using an omnitool, opened the panel on the bot's back to access its artificial intelligence computer core. The maintenance bot was designed to remove a broken galact pump when it was damaged beyond repair by lifting the pump off the ground and zapping it with a beam that dematerialized the pump.

The saboteur modified the programming of the bot so that it would mistake fully functional pumps for broken ones. The saboteur, having completed his work, activated the maintenance bot. It was at that moment that Gilbert noticed the wavering of the saboteur's cloaked shield on the back of the bot.

"Aoléon, what is that wavering up there on that huge robot? It looks like a cloaked form — similar to the sentinel."

Aoléon gazed upward at the maintenance bot and spotted the cloaked form clinging to the back of the robot. "That is him! Let us get him!" cried Aoléon as she ran over to the base of the large maintenance bot and began to climb up to the saboteur. The saboteur changed directions

and began to climb back up to the head of the robot where there was a cockpit for optional manual control of the bot.

"Zoot! Quick! He is going to take control of the bot itself!" cried Aoléon. Zoot scampered up to the robot and jumped onto one of its legs. Zoot then shot his long tongue out like a grappling hook, and using the suction cup end of it, stuck it to the outside of the bot's head. Using his tongue as a rope, Zoot swung himself up to the outside of the canopy and scampered quickly to near where the saboteur was sitting at the controls. The saboteur didn't notice Zoot at first because he was struggling with the controls, trying to reactivate the bot. Finally, he was able to get it moving, and with a lurch, the bot started to move forward, knocking Aoléon off its leg and sending her flying to the ground. Zoot momentarily lost his grip and swung down again, clinging to the outside of the bot with his suction-cup tongue.

Up and down…up and down…the pumps and drone riders went without ceasing. The giant sabotaged maintenance bot sprang to life, swooping down row upon row of pumps like a Tyrannosaurus Rex looking for a meal.

Spotting its first victim, the maintenance bot scooped up the galact pump into the air while its maintenance drones still hung on, clinging to the controls. The bot fired a beam at the pump and vaporized it.

Aoléon watched in horror as the maintenance bot found another pump — its next snack. It grabbed the pump with its tentacled arms and lifted it high up into the air, its worker drone dangling from a single arm and holding on for dear life. Then it hit the pump and drones with the beam. All that was left was a puff of smoke, which it expelled with a loud mechanical BURP. The maintenance bot continued floating down the rows upon rows of galact pumps, looking for its next morsel. Both the pumps and the drones eyed each other silently after the maintenance bot passed, wondering which one would be next.

Zoot shot his suction-cup tongue out and used it like a grappling hook to hoist himself up to the head of the bot where he could attack the saboteur. In the struggle between Zoot and the saboteur, the robot went haywire, moving in random directions, scooping up some galact pumps with Martian drones clinging to them and vaporizing them.

One of the drones hopped down off his galact pump and communicated to the others telepathically. After a third drone worker was zapped along with his pump, they grouped together and attacked the maintenance bot in force. Hundreds of drones swarmed the enormous maintenance bot, climbing up its tentacles and clinging to its head; although, most were thrown off as the bot flailed about and continued its rampage.

ⓞⓞⓞ

Deimos who could hear the explosions, panicked and came running from another part of the factory. He saw the disaster unfolding before him and called his superior on the holokron to report. As his boss began shouting orders at him over the ruckus, one of the pumps exploded in a great ball of fire, then another, and another. Struck by the explosion, Deimos slammed into the wall.

"Oh, no! It looks like we are too late!" Aoléon exhaled as she took in the view of fire and explosive damage to the Galactworks. "We need to find my father. He is close by. I can sense him."

Gilbert followed Aoléon as she moved through the burning wreck of galact pumps. Finally they reached the central control area. At first he didn't see anything, but after a moment of searching, they located Deimos lying on the floor, writhing in pain.

"Ahh, father! I came to warn you!" cried Aoléon.

"You are too late, my child," Deimos let out an agonizing groan.

"Just lie still." Aoléon closed her eyes and gently placed her hands over her father. A glowing light appeared from her hands, and after a few moments, she opened her eyes again. She focused on the healing process as the robot continued to rampage throughout the facility. She heard Zoot call out with a loud "BRRREEET" and looked up to see the saboteur falling through the air.

The struggle with Zoot and the erratic motion of the bot caused the saboteur to slip and fall out of the canopy forty-five feet to the ground where he collapsed on impact and lay unmoving. The robot finally came to a halt among the smoking ruins of the galact pumps. Zoot leapt down to find Aoléon and Gilbert.

Gilbert saw the saboteur fall from the bot and rushed over to the body that now lay on the ground. He carefully removed the helmet of the saboteur and gasped when he saw its face.

"Aoléon, quick! You have to see this!" Gilbert called out.

"What is it? My father is hurt and needs my attention."

"It's the saboteur…he's a she!"

"What?"

"Not only that, but I think it's your old friend from class."

Aoléon rushed over to Gilbert who was leaning over the unmoving form of the saboteur. A Martian girl lay before them with her eyes shut as if she were sleeping.

Aoléon gasped. "Oh my! Charm!"

"Should I wake her up? She has some explaining to do," Gilbert said, as he shook her. Charm sputtered and opened her eyes.

"It is you!" cried Aoléon. "But why? Why would you do such a thing?"

"A-a-a...," Charm sputtered. "Aoléon, I am very sorry... they gave me no choice. My family...they were captured by the Xiocrom. They told me that if I did not do as they said, my family would be nullified."

"The Xiocrom told you to sabotage the Galactworks?"

"Yes!" And as she said the words, she fired a psionic blast at Aoléon and Gilbert, knocking them back, and then disappeared in a flash of light as she phased out of the chamber.

"Deus ex machina!" Aoléon cried. "She phased!"

"Can we go after her?"

"There is no way of knowing to where she phased," Aoléon explained. She touched Gilbert's shoulder lightly. "Come on, we must get my father home. He is weak and needs rest."

Aoléon and Gilbert helped lift Deimos to his feet. "Come, I will take you home." Aoléon reached out her other hand to Gilbert and Zoot. A flash of white light blinded Gilbert as they phased out of the chamber together. Gilbert felt himself being compressed as if moving under water at a great depth. He opened his eyes to see that they were back in Aoléon's home, safe at last. Aoléon and Phobos tended to Deimos while Gilbert, who was exhausted from their adventure, fell asleep.

The next morning, Gilbert and Aoléon left for class at the Martian Space Academy. She seemed tired, having spent part of the night healing her father who fortunately had made a quick recovery. Despite the tragedy that happened yesterday at the Galactworks, Aoléon seemed her normal upbeat, if exhausted, self.

"Today is the big day for me," Aoléon exclaimed as they phase-jumped in front of the Martian Space Academy. "Today I will take my pilot's exam."

"That's wonderful! Are you nervous?"

"A little…come on. We are going to be late for class."

Classes went without a hitch. Gilbert attended astrophysics, interstellar navigation, and a class on fusion reactor core maintenance. Gilbert and Aoléon ran into Charm's friends in two of their classes, but Gilbert noticed that Charm was nowhere to be found. He wasn't surprised, but he held out hope that they might run into her so that he could confront her about what happened at the Galactworks.

Throughout the day, Gilbert had the chance to meet more of Aoléon's friends. Lunae, Nili, Zephyria, and Dao joined Aoléon and Gilbert at their table for midday consumption. They were eager to hear about Gilbert's life on his farm in Nebraska. Iani and Arsinoes were in Aoléon's temporal mechanics class and kept making jokes by levitating the teacher's chair out from under him. Apollinaris, Aeolis, Arnon, Ascuris, and Aetheria were sixth-year cadets. As they passed her in the hall, they congratulated Aoléon on her performance in the psi-ball match.

HOLLOW MOON
CHAPTER ELEVEN

MARTIAN SPACE ACADEMY
MARTIAN MEGALOPOLIS
OLYMPUS MONS
PLANET MARS

When class let out, Aoléon turned excitedly to Gilbert. "It is time for my pilot's exam. If I pass, I will be allowed to enter the academy's pilot training program. After I graduate, they will permit me to join the Martian Intergalactic Explorational Fleet."

"That shouldn't be a problem after the flying you did back on Earth!" Gilbert beamed.

"I hope not," she said blushing a slightly darker hue of turquoise.

They entered the hangar bay where one of the flight instructors was waiting. Gilbert noticed that he had a special kind of spacesuit that appeared to be of military issue, albeit a Martian kind. He was standing next to a saucer of a type

Gilbert hadn't seen before. This one was much larger and sleeker than Aoléon's saucer.

"Ready to begin the testing, sir," Aoléon said as she waved her straightened arm in a circular, outward spiral motion, which Gilbert surmised was the Martian salute.

"Good," he replied. "Will your guest be coming with us?"

"If it is not a problem, sir. He is a visiting exchange student who is here to observe our training methods. His name is Gilbert."

"Nice to meet you, Gilbert," the flight instructor said, nodding his head. "Welcome to the Martian Space Academy Pilot Training Program. My name is Instructor Nezbat. Aoléon, please take your station aboard the vessel and walk me through the preflight procedures."

"Yes sir," responded Aoléon. They followed the instructor into the ship.

"I will start by doing a preflight systems check," Aoléon said as she waved her hand over the console to activate the ship's systems. The control panel lit up, and several holographic displays sprang to life, projecting tiny floating images of Martian glyphs above the console. The system responded by telling them that everything was in working order. "Now I will power up the fusion reactor and bring the gravimetric displacement field generators on line," Aoléon said confidently.

The ship whirred to life and began to hum as a glow emanated from all around the ship. "I have established telepathic contact with the onboard AI. The ship is ready, and all systems are fully functional, instructor."

"Good. Now take her up slowly and exit the hangar bay."

"Yes, sir," said Aoléon. She waved her hand over a holographic image of the ship hovering in front of her. The ship lifted from the platform and flew slowly out through the opening of the hangar bay. Aoléon slowed the ship to a halt, awaiting her next order.

"Now I want you to fly a loop around the megalopolis," said the instructor.

Aoléon, using her telepathic link to the ship, sped the craft forward. It accelerated, climbing high over the megalopolis. Gilbert could see crowds of Martians down below traveling back and forth on ambulatories linking various buildings, flowing like streams of ants from an anthill. They flew over sparkling silver spires and golden atriums with transparent metal that shone like gems in the Martian sunlight. Aoléon guided the ship into one of the main traffic streams, merging into the flow of traffic with hundreds of other ships.

"Well done," affirmed Instructor Nezbat. "Now take the ship into orbit and circle around the planet."

"Yes, sir!" responded Aoléon as she again moved her hand gently, taking the ship upward toward the dome of the megalopolis. "Requesting deactivation of the cloaking shield," Aoléon said to the Martian Space Traffic Control.

"Permission granted," replied the space traffic controller. "Maintain your current course heading."

The saucer flew out at high speed over the cliff surrounding the crater that formed the enormous caldera of Olympus Mons. In less than two minutes, they passed over the entire length of the giant Vallis Marineris canyon system, which was more than three thousand miles long. The ship accelerated rapidly, climbed vertically, and headed into space. As they entered Martian orbit, they passed the Phobos moon and saw an enormous mothership hovering behind it, larger than the moon itself.

"Zoikers! Look at that thing!" Gilbert said. "The ship is bigger than that moon over there."

"I believe it to be the Sphaira, a galaxy-class mothership, serving as one of the main base-ships for the Martian Galactic Fleet. It is rare to see a base-ship so close to home," replied Instructor Nezbat.

"That is bigger than huge!" exclaimed Gilbert.

"The largest mothership we have is the Megál Mitéra (Gilbert heard the translation 'Big Mother' in his head), which is an intergalactic-class mothership. It is more than nine hundred of your Terran miles in diameter. The entire Martian megalopolis on Olympus Mons could fit inside its volume."

"Zoikers!"

A holokron suddenly materialized and began projecting a holokronic image before them. Floating in space before them, they could see the holokronic projection of a Martian

man's face. He appeared to be some kind of high-ranking officer in the Martian Galactic Fleet.

"ATTENTION TRAINING VESSEL. THIS IS GALACTIC FLEET ADMIRAL NOKU COMMANDING THE MOTHERSHIP SPHAIRA...[static transmission interruption] ...ENTERING RESTRICTED SPACE. YOU MUST...[static transmission interruption]...HEADING IMMEDIATELY. DO NOT...[more static interruptions]... CLOSER OR YOU WILL BE DE..." The message was cut off permanently by interference as if jammed at the source.

"We better turn around," said Instructor Nezbat.

"Understood, sir. Changing our heading," replied Aoléon.

They seem to be conducting military maneuvers. I am surprised that I was not informed, commented the instructor telepathically as if he were thinking out loud to himself. *This is most unusual.*

Gilbert was surprised to hear his thoughts so clearly. Suddenly another holokronic projection appeared. The apparition of Pax floated before them. Gilbert recognized Pax from when they ran into him on Mars. It was Pax who had first warned them about the Luminon's plans to invade Earth. It was Pax who had urged both of them to investigate the Luminon. He also remembered seeing numerous holokronic projections announcing Pax as the leader of the rebellion. He was the number one most wanted Martian by the Xiocrom and the Luminon.

"A-A-A-A-Aoléon, you m-m-must investigate the Phobos m-m-m-m-moon. Ph-Ph-Ph-hobos is a key to the Luminon's p-p-p-p-plans to conquer both Earth and Mars," said Pax, his voice becoming distorted in the transmission. The signal interference was causing the transmission to hiccup; an artificially delayed stuttering of his speech made his voice sound like rushing water while his image wavered and broke with signal noise.

"What is this?!" exclaimed Instructor Nezbat as he reached for his sidearm. "Aoléon, are you working for the resistance?"

"What? No!" Aoléon cried. "I am just a cadet in training!"

"Just hold it right there! I am going to turn you in to the Xiocrom," exclaimed Instructor Nezbat as he drew his disruptor pistol and pointed it at Aoléon.

"A-A-A-Aoléon, Ph-Ph-Ph-Phobos is the k-key! You must…G-G-G-Go to Ph-Ph-Phobos—" With a flash, the Pax holokron disappeared.

Their ship lurched, buffeted by a shock wave that sent Aoléon, Gilbert, and Instructor Nezbat flying through the air. They crashed into the saucer bulkhead wall. Gilbert tasted blood in his mouth and shook his head a couple times, trying to clear the stars from his eyes. Gilbert cleared his head in time to see waves of energy appear in front and behind them. Four tall beings in black spacesuits and carrying plasma weapons materialized.

Instructor Nezbat fired at one of the tall, black-suited beings and instantly disintegrated him. The other three beings returned fire and struck Instructor Nezbat, vaporizing him. Gilbert stared at the place where the instructor had just been a moment ago; only a dark shadow on the hull remained. He glanced at Aoléon in time to see her make a couple of quick circular movements with her left hand. A blue beam of energy shot from her palm and struck the two of the four attackers. The two invaders flew across the length of the ship and slammed against a bulkhead wall. Their outer suits were singed as if burned by an intense laser beam. As Aoléon attempted to combat the remaining beings, a stasis field materialized around both of them.

Aoléon and Gilbert froze in place. "What's going on?" Gilbert cried. He was completely paralyzed. He could only breathe, move his mouth, and turn his eyes.

"I do not know!" Aoléon replied. She attempted to squirm but couldn't, her body frozen in a stasis field.

The two dark-suited beings that remained conscious exchanged sideward glances. They quickly conversed with each other, producing strange guttural hissing noises. "Sssshiaass shakkka sskkhhhshhh." The two invaders picked themselves up from the floor and took guard positions, standing on either side of Aoléon and Gilbert.

Gilbert felt another lurch as the ship began to move. Normally, the ship's gravimetric field cancelled all inertial forces. Aoléon could now sense outside movement from within the ship. That told her the ship's primary drive had been disabled, and an unknown outside force was in control of the vessel.

They must have the ship in some kind of tractor beam because no one is piloting it, Aoléon communicated telepathically to Gilbert.

Because he could do nothing else, Gilbert closely examined the two beings standing guard over him. The shorter of the two stood eight-and-a-half feet tall, with an incredibly muscular build. The tallest one seemed to be at least twelve feet tall. They had to crouch and bend over to stand inside the ship because their helmets and upper backs touched the ceiling of the saucer craft. Their faces were concealed behind tinted helmet visors, and they clutched large disruptor rifles in their gloved hands. The strangest part about them was their feet. They were oversized and had what looked like huge claws or talons coming from their boots where their toes should have been.

Aoléon, who are they, and where are they taking us?

Draconian warriors. They are taking us to the Phobos moon.

How do you know for sure?

I read their thoughts.

Why would they take us to your moon?

I do not know, but we are about to find out. I am going to try to contact Bizwat telepathically and tell him that we have been captured. Maybe he can help us.

The pizza guy?! Are you sure about that?

He is our best hope.

That's just wonderful, Gilbert thought. *We're doomed.*

Several minutes passed, and the ship came to a halt. Draconian guards entered the ship. One activated a small device that caused the stasis fields around Aoléon and Gilbert to levitate. The duo floated out of the ship horizontally and feet first with the guards following them.

As they exited the saucer, Gilbert looked up to find himself inside an enormous rock cavern. The walls snaked upwards (he guessed toward the surface of the moon) where the mouth to the entrance was blocked by a cloaking force field designed to both protect and conceal the entrance by making it appear to be solid rock on the outside.

The inside of the cavern had been flattened into an enormous docking bay. Hundreds of cigar-tube- and pea-pod-shaped ships of varying sizes hovered before them, docked in rows. Gilbert looked up to see several balls of plasma floating near the ceiling. The plasma balls, like tiny suns, gave off natural sunlight. Across the landing bay tarmac and between the ships, stood a battalion of troops in full battle armor. Some were at least eight feet tall, and others stood even taller.

Draconian warriors! cried Aoléon telepathically. *This is an invasion force!*

Oh my! Gilbert took a close look at the Draconians who were guarding them. A noxious feeling crept over him. *These guys make an NBA team seem puny by comparison!*

These are truly awesome creatures to behold, he thought. Gilbert remembered Plutarch Xenocrates' lecture on the Draconians — how they were the oldest species in the galaxy and the first to achieve interstellar space flight almost four-and-a-half billion years ago. "Intergalactic bullies of the universe," a Martian girl had declared. "Party-poopers of the galaxy," someone else had said.

The creatures moved swiftly and silently with military precision. The Draconians wore either a uniform, protective armor, or nothing at all. The ones without clothes were completely covered with scales. Speckles of dark browns and oranges mixed with lighter brown-and-beige-hued scales gave some a freckled appearance. Lumps of tiny, horn-like protrusions sprouted from their heads, running vertically from the forehead area over the tops of their heads and down the backs of their necks. Their noses were long, flattened against their faces and culminated in a diminutive snout that featured two slitted nostrils. When they opened their mouths, Gilbert could see a fairly even row of backward-facing serrated teeth.

Their hands contained three long fingers with an opposing thumb, ending in long claw-like talons. Although most were

tailless, a few of the higher-ranking officers possessed tails. (Gilbert identified the officers as the ones who seemed to be issuing orders.) They mainly kept their tails coiled; a few would occasionally extend and twitch their tails back and forth while hissing commands at their underlings.

The Draconians had oversized, bulging eyes with slitted pupils that protruded from their foreheads. They reminded Gilbert of the dinosaurs — possibly ones that may have evolved into a humanoid form. Gilbert had had an interest in dinosaurs since he was a small child, and he imagined that these creatures were essentially bipedal, intelligent, and technologically advanced velociraptors. The thought sent a chill down his spine.

ⓞ ⓞ ⓞ

PHOBOS MOON
ABOVE PLANET MARS

Draconian guards marched alongside Aoléon and Gilbert as they floated along, helplessly frozen in their stasis fields. They passed between two large starships on their way toward the rear of the hangar bay. Gilbert noticed that the massive hangar bay was filled with rows of hovering cigar-shaped spacecraft, with the largest equal in length to a Nimitz-class aircraft carrier. The ship closest to him gave off a very deep thrumming sound that was more easily felt than heard.

They made their way across the docking bay toward a portal on the far side. Two guards stationed on either side of the portal moved to allow the procession to pass through. All Gilbert could hear were his own heavy breathing and the hum of the force field surrounding him. Every so often, the silence would be broken by a guttural "sssssshhhkiaaaa, sssssshhhkkkkkaaa, shkaaaiaaassss" sound. A horrible rasping noise emerged from the helmets of the Draconian warriors when they spoke to one another.

That must be their language, Gilbert thought. *They're probably trying to determine who gets to eat us first.* "I think we may be in a cave deep inside your moon," Gilbert accidentally spoke out loud to Aoléon.

"SSSS-SILENCE!" A raspy hissing voice shouted at him. "OR I EAT YOU!"

Gilbert felt chills go down his back. He tried to turn his head, but the stasis field immobilized his entire body.

Gilbert heard Aoléon's voice in his head: *They prey upon fear. You must transform your emotions. Weakness will only embolden them.*

Adrenaline coursed through Gilbert's veins like burning plasma. He felt cold and began to shake uncontrollably. White flashes appeared before his eyes. He realized that he was hyperventilating. With great effort and concentration, he controlled his breathing. It seemed to be working because the stars eventually cleared from his eyes.

You are doing well. Aoléon reassured him telepathically. *We will find a way to escape. Do not lose hope.*

They floated through another large cavern into a hovering transport train that floated inside a tubular track. The transport sped off down a tunnel, winding around and dipping like a roller coaster. They passed through another deep cavern. In the center, enormous stalactite-like buildings stood carved out of moon rock. The structures stretched from floor to ceiling and were several hundred feet high. On platforms below, battalions of Draconian warriors prepared for battle. They passed through another tunnel into a smaller chamber where Gilbert could see reptiloids sunning themselves under a floating ball of plasma that resembled a tiny sun.

They must be cold-blooded...just like lizards on Earth! Gilbert thought. And they have made their own artificial suns to keep themselves warm underground. The way the reptiloids bowed before the artificial sun sparked another thought in Gilbert's mind. *It looks as if they are not just warming themselves. They are worshiping it!*

It is ironic how a species that worships the stars lives in darkness, underground, replied Aoléon telepathically.

The hovering train came to a halt. They were moved into a chamber while still suspended by the stasis field. Several of the guards left the room, but two remained. Suddenly a beam of energy surrounded them. A portal opened in the ceiling above. Gilbert gasped for air. He felt a jolt hit him in the stomach, and he blacked out. Gilbert awoke to find himself lying in the center of a giant colosseum with a Draconian standing over him.

Gilbert gazed upward in a semiconscious state. A crowd of thousands of jeering reptiloids slowly came into focus; the roar of the crowd crashed over him. Near the center of the colosseum, a throne set apart from the crowd held a monstrously huge, powdery-white scaled Draconian. A great hissing voice pierced the thrum of the crowd, and a hush fell. The enormous Draconian stood and motioned toward Gilbert and Aoléon.

A Ciakar! Aoléon cried telepathically. She suddenly felt ill and began to shake.

"Bring forth the prisoners," the Ciakar commanded. (Actually, Gilbert heard it make a guttural hissing sound. But given what happened next, he surmised that is what it said.)

Two guards standing beside Aoléon and Gilbert deactivated their stasis fields and led them toward the throne, which sat atop the thirty-five-foot wall that surrounded the arena. The guards prodded them forward until they reached a spot near the throne where they forced them to kneel.

"Oh great Draco Prime, we present our prisoners. Two spies — a hu-mon and a Martian girl. What is thy bidding?"

"Throw them to the Sukr'ath. They shall entertain us with their ssss–screams!" the Draco leader commanded with a wave of its massive arm. A cacophony of hisses and thundering cheers erupted from the crowd and reverberated off the cavern walls.

"Sukr'ath! Sukr'ath! Sukr'ath!" chanted the crowd.

The guards bowed. They stood and handed Aoléon and Gilbert each a weapon, a staff with two large, shiny blades attached to each end. The weapon Gilbert held was enormous, almost twice his own height. (Obviously fit for an eight-foot-tall reptiloid and not for a four-foot eleven-inch tall human boy.) He grasped it in his hands expecting it to be extremely heavy but was surprised to discover how light it felt. Then he remembered where he was — Phobos, a medium-sized asteroid moon. *Must be the reduced gravity of this moon.*

Slowly the guards exited through a portal concealed in the colosseum's high wall that surrounded the arena pit. It promptly sealed behind them leaving no visible means for escape. Gilbert glanced down at his weapon and then looked up at Aoléon who seemed too preoccupied or frightened to notice. He watched her for a moment and then shook her gently on the shoulder. Aoléon just stood there frozen, staring into space, not even bothering to reach for her weapon. *She is in shock,* he thought. "Aoléon, wake up!"

All of a sudden an enormous portal opened. A platform emerged from below, lifting forth a gargantuan monster. A loud cheer erupted from the crowd. Gilbert gripped his weapon tighter. Stay calm! he told himself.

The monster rose to at least forty feet high, its body covered with spiky horns. It had four enormous muscular arms with gigantic clawed hands. Two stout legs supporting the beast bent backwards at the knee. Atop its head sat eight hideous eyes — four on the left and four on the right, tightly stacked on top of one another. The Sukr'ath opened

its gigantic mouth, revealing many rows of sharp fangs, some as long as broadswords. It let out a thunderous roar, totally drowning out the thrum of the crowd. The walls of the great colosseum shook. The stasis field surrounding it dropped, and the great monster charged forward, taking giant lumbering steps.

Gilbert tried to run, but the reduced gravity of the Martian moon gave his legs incredible strength and carried him high up into the air. He was not yet accustomed to the light, micro-gravity. Each step unexpectedly became a giant bounding leap, which would have been impossible on Earth or even on Mars. He leapt backward about twenty feet and tumbled to the ground. He turned and saw Aoléon standing frozen with fear in the same place he had left her, and he watched in horror as the giant moved toward her.

The Sukr'ath reached down with one of its immense clawed hands and scooped up Aoléon. It lifted her horribly, slowly toward its gigantic, tooth-filled mouth. *I must save her*, Gilbert thought. With a sudden bolt of courage, Gilbert took another running leap. This time he was ready for his flight. He sailed through the air, heading directly for the monster and Aoléon. The one advantage Gilbert had over the monster was that he was quick, and it was slow and clumsy. Gilbert timed his leap perfectly so that he landed on top of the arm that held Aoléon before the monster even realized he was there.

Swinging his weapon with all his might, Gilbert stabbed the monster's hand. The blade plunged deep into its flesh. The Sukr'ath let out a terrible roar and dropped Aoléon. She fell thirty feet to the ground. (Luckily due to the

Phobos moon's light gravity, her landing was soft.) Gilbert leapt off the monster's arm and landed beside Aoléon. He quickly helped her to her feet.

"Thank you!" wheezed Aoléon.

"No time to talk. Let's find a way out of here!" he cried.

"B-but—, i-it is impossible…," Aoléon stammered, still shaking.

"Aoléon, listen! Nothing is impossible. You proved that to me."

Gilbert rapidly scanned the walls of the colosseum but found no means of escape. Taking Aoléon in his arms (which was relatively easy given the greatly reduced gravity), he leapt to the top of the wall surrounding the arena. The crowd went crazy, screaming, hissing, and yelling while the nearby mob of reptiloids grabbed Gilbert and Aoléon and tossed them back into the arena.

The Sukr'ath, now even angrier than before, charged at the duo, intending to stomp them to jelly. Gilbert grabbed Aoléon again and sprang out of the way, barely missing the charging monster as it collided with the towering wall of the colosseum. The impact struck the air like a shot from a cannon and shook the ground like an earthquake.

Aoléon motioned for Gilbert to set her down and closed her eyes in deep concentration. Blue orbs of light appeared around the head of the monster, causing the Sukr'ath to stumble and waver. After a few moments of lumbering around the arena like a drunken dinosaur, the Sukr'ath collapsed with a thunderous boom and lay on the ground snoring. Gilbert realized that Aoléon must have used her psionic power to put the monster to sleep.

"Brilliant!" he shouted gleefully. "We have a saying on Earth: the bigger they are, the harder they fall! You just proved that."

Aoléon smiled.

Silence fell over the crowd. Anger and confusion spread over their saurian faces. They hissed, they screeched, and they growled. They sounded like thousands of snakes curled up and ready to strike. The Draco Prime rose from his throne and with a wave of his arm drew silence. With another wave, several Draconian guards emerged, took their weapons, and led them back to the gravtube platform from which they had emerged.

After reactivating the stasis fields around Aoléon and Gilbert, the Draconian guards placed the duo in the center of the gravtube ready for transport. The rushing sound of the crowd ceased as the portal to the colosseum shut and they were whisked away, farther down into the bowels of the reptiloid moon base.

Now back in their holding cell, Aoléon and Gilbert were placed in stasis fields, and all the guards except two left the room. Some time passed, and Gilbert dreaded what might happen next.

The door to their cell opened, and a being Gilbert immediately recognized as the powdery-white-scaled Draconian leader entered the room. The creature's presence sent shivers down Gilbert's spine.

Now I see why they are known as the dragon race! Gilbert thought. *This must be one of their royalty.*

The Ciakar peered down at them for several moments, gazing into them with its intense eyes without saying a word. Finally it spoke. "My name is unpronounceable in your tongue. If misspoken, I would be forced to eat you on the spot. Suffice to say, I am Caput Draconis, or head dragon, a member of the Draconian ruling caste and commander of this installation. I expect you to answer my questions truthfully, or you will be eaten alive. Who sent you?" spat the Ciakar with an impatient flick of its tail.

"N-no one s-sent us. W-we were on a r-routine t-training m-mission," Aoléon stuttered, her hands and body shaking slightly in the stasis field.

The eyes of the Ciakar lit up. What Gilbert thought had been a cape on his back momentarily stretched out into dragon-like wings and then folded along his back. "Liar! You were sent to spy on us," hissed the Ciakar. "The question is *by whom?* You were not ordered by your military command…that is for certain. So, who ordered you to fly around Phobos?"

"N-no one s-sent us, s-sir," Aoléon quivered. "I am a c-cadet in the M-Martian S-Space Academy, and I was t-taking my flight test when we were boarded."

"Are you aware that I am telepathic?" the Ciakar spoke, addressing Aoléon directly. "Not to the same degree that you are, of course, but enough to read the primitive hu-mon boy's mind. I already scanned his thoughts, and he knows very little. But *you* my child…*you* are able *to block me.* Perhaps you will answer me honestly after you watch me *eat* your little hu-mon friend?"

The Ciakar moved toward Gilbert and swiped its clawed hand across Gilbert's chest. The stasis field around him dropped. Reaching down, he single-handedly grabbed Gilbert by his neck and lifted him off his feet into the air up to its head level. The Draco clutched Gilbert's throat tightly, making it almost impossible to breathe. "There is nothing that is as delicious and melts in your mouth like a hu-mon child."

"Ahhkkkkk!" Gilbert choked, trying to let out a scream. The blood slowly drained from his face. His eyes filled with tears. The Ciakar examined Gilbert with cold, lifeless eyes. It was as if Gilbert were peering into the face of death itself. Gilbert's stomach sank as he realized that this creature could indeed eat him alive without a second thought.

"I am more than four thousand years old by your Earth calendar. Your great ancestors used to worship me as a god. So do not think for an instant that I can be fooled by your lies."

"Wait!" Aoléon screamed. "I will tell you whatever you want to know. Just do not hurt him!"

"Who sent you then?" The piercing slits for eyes flashed with intensity as he spoke. The grip upon Gilbert's neck loosened a bit, enabling him to take a breath.

Aoléon took a moment to scan the Ciakar's mind before responding. "Uhh…the resistance. They sent us to, umm… spy on you and to find out what your plans were," Aoléon spoke, making up a story that she thought might soothe the angry Ciakar and buy them more time.

"How many of you are there?" The Ciakar lowered Gilbert slightly but didn't set him on the ground.

"Not many left, sir. The Luminon has captured most of us and only a handful remain," Aoléon said, becoming more comfortable with her fabrication.

"What do you know about our plans to invade Earth?"

"Nothing, sir."

"Liar! Shall I take a bite out of your little hu-mon friend? Shall I tear his flesh with one of my claws? It would give me *great* pleasure to hear him scream."

"No! Please no! I am being honest with you, I swear! All we knew was that you were planning an invasion. That is all!"

The Ciakar peered at Gilbert, clutched in its hand. "You are nothing but a pitiful sub-creature — genetically engineered as a slave race eons ago to service us. For countless ages, hu-mons worshipped the Draco as gods and constructed pyramids in our name! Soon, once again, the hu-mons will be forced to serve us as they did in ancient times. For we are your overlords! You are the first to bear witness to the new world order where Draconians will once again rule hu-mon kind!"

"You're nothing more than a fallen angel." Gilbert realized that this could be the end of him. He was incredibly frightened. If fright were a fish, his would be a whale. Except whales are not fish. But they're big! And that is the point. Gilbert was really, truly, and most assuredly frightened. But something churned deeper inside of him, and his fear began to turn to rage. His primordial survival instinct took over; a rush of adrenaline greatly increased his strength.

"We will tell you whatever you want to know, just do not nullify us," Aoléon pleaded, tears streaming down her blue cheeks.

The Ciakar lifted Gilbert's head a bit closer so that they were face to face, and it examined him closely. As it did so, Gilbert noticed the air wavering behind the Draco. Two flashes briefly lit up the room, and the guards standing by the door crumpled to the ground. The Ciakar snapped its enormous head around, distracted for a moment by the sound of the guards collapsing. Gilbert kicked the great Ciakar in the head with all his strength, causing it to drop him. Scampering backwards on all fours, Gilbert tried to put as much distance as possible between himself and the Ciakar.

The Ciakar ignored Gilbert and searched the room. It saw the two dead Draconian guards lying next to their severed heads. Its eyes tightened. It realized it was in danger, but it was already too late. Gilbert saw another waver of light directly behind it. A beam of light flashed, neatly slicing through the giant Ciakar's neck. The beam disappeared as quickly as it had appeared. And, just for a moment, Gilbert thought that he might have imagined it.

Just as he decided that he had imagined it, the Ciakar opened its mouth to speak but instead produced gurgling and rasping noises. The creature's arms reached for its head. But before they could grasp it, the head toppled from its shoulders and hit the ground, rolling across the floor. The giant, headless Ciakar collapsed.

Gilbert felt both relieved and horrified. Then realizing that by some strange miracle his life had been spared, he cheered silently. The brief respite of jubilation ended as quickly as it began. It was replaced once again by fear as he realized that whatever had just killed the great white Draconian leader was still in the room with him.

A moment passed. Gilbert saw another shimmer. A ghostly silhouette appeared, standing over the lifeless corpse of the great white Draco leader. From it, a being in an armored suit emerged.

"*Did someone here order a pizza?*" the dark-suited figure queried as he removed his helmet, revealing a youthful Martian face that Gilbert recognized instantly.

"Bizwat!"

"You found us! Thank the Creator!" cried Aoléon.

"That was really cool!" Gilbert wheezed, his shoulders slumping in exhaustion. "I mean…how did you do that!?"

"Procyon trade secret, my curious Terran friend. Come. Time to leave." He moved over to Aoléon, deactivated her stasis field, and helped her down. Bizwat removed a pizza-shaped device from his back and slid it gently underneath the Draco's corpse.

"It would seem that I received your message just in time."

"You did! We are forever indebted to you," cried Aoléon, tears trickling down her cheek.

"That's not a pizza you have there, is it? Cause if it is, I'm starved!" Gilbert gestured toward Bizwat, grinning widely.

Bizwat chuckled as he finished setting the device underneath the Draco's body. "It is just a little slice of Armageddon for our scaly friends. An antimatter demolition munitions set with a motion-trembler trigger switch. When they move the body, they will get a surprise in the form of a 1.2 exajoule antimatter explosion — about 250 megatons to you Terrans. I hope you like your lizard meat well done on your pizza because when this baby goes off it is ECCLBT."

"Um, okay…I know this is important…so what's ECCLBT?"

"It is a technical term we use in the Martian special forces. It means, 'Extra-Crispy-Critter-Lizard-Barbecue-Time,'" said Bizwat. "Just like the oroboros, we are going to feed these serpents their tails."

"I told you Bizwat is not just an average pizza delivery guy," Aoléon beamed.

"Um, yeah—," Gilbert said laughing. "I see that now."

"Enough talk. I have a ship in orbit. We should phase there directly." Bizwat grabbed Gilbert and Aoléon, and they phase-jumped out of the chamber to his ship, which was hovering cloaked above Phobos.

☉☉☉

BIZWAT'S SAUCER
SPACE, PHOBOS MOON
ABOVE PLANET MARS

ow did you get captured by the reptiloids?" Bizwat inquired as they settled inside the cockpit of his saucer.

"I was taking my pilot's exam, making a run around Phobos when we were boarded. They must have thought we were spying on them, so they took us captive."

"Procyon intel had no idea the base was there. Now we know where they were hiding and what they plan to do," said Bizwat.

"Yeah, invade Earth: my home," replied Gilbert.

"Thanks to you two, we have now destroyed the reptiloid base. Had you not stumbled upon it, we may never have done so. Pilot's exam, heh!"

"We destroyed the base?" asked Gilbert.

"Patience, my young Terran friend. Any moment now they will discover the body of their leader…and then, αντίο μου φίλους, το κόμμα είναι πάνω από."

"I don't understand."

"As they say back on your world — 'Goodbye my friends! The party is over.'"

Gilbert smiled. Bizwat turned and began his preflight check as the saucer's systems spun up.

"Gilbert, I am so very sorry for getting you into this," Aoléon said, tears running down her cheeks. "I thought we would be eaten for sure."

"It's not your fault. You had no idea that we were going to be captured." Gilbert took her hand and held it in his, comforting her. "You do have quite a knack for finding trouble though," he chuckled, giving her hand a little squeeze.

"If Aoléon's ability for finding trouble could somehow be captured, you would have a weapon of mass destruction so deadly that not even bacteria would survive," Bizwat said, laughing.

Aoléon perked up a little and managed a smile, wiping some of the tears off her face with her sleeve. "You should have seen Gilbert when he saved me from the giant Sukr'ath."

"You battled a Sukr'ath?"

"He did. And because of him, I am still alive," Aoléon said looking at Gilbert.

"Even for a Procyon, that is impressive!"

Gilbert blushed. "Well, you put the thing to sleep!" Gilbert laughed, patting Aoléon on the shoulder. "I couldn't have made it without your help." They both chuckled.

Gilbert recoiled, a surge of energy prickling up his spine. A burst of blinding light filled the craft. Gilbert cleared the white spots from his eyes as he peered out from the saucer just in time to see an enormous explosion rip in half the thirteen-mile-long Phobos moon. The saucer quickly accelerated and sped out of harm's way from the oncoming shock wave of moon rock debris and hot plasma.

"You destroyed the moon!" Aoléon exclaimed.

"And the reptiloid base along with it," Gilbert said after he regained his breath.

"Would you have preferred that we leave the Draconian invasion force intact?" Bizwat inquired.

"Umm…no, but it is just that I was quite fond of that moon…my mother was named after it," Aoléon said solemnly.

Bizwat grunted.

"Now that we have some time, I wanted to mention something to you. These creatures that captured us…I have seen something similar to them before," said Gilbert.

"When?"

"When I first arrived on Mars and we ran into the Luminess. Just before she entered my mind, I saw her face briefly transform into what looked to me like a lizard. And then, when we were above the Luminon's throne room, I saw his head transform into something that looked like a velociraptor. Having come very close to being eaten by one on that moon, I am now pretty sure they are both Draconians in disguise."

"May I share your thoughts?" asked Bizwat.

"Umm…yeah, sure," said Gilbert.

Bizwat scanned Gilbert's memories of the two events. "Compelling, although hardly conclusive. They are known to have shape-shifting abilities. But, given that we are a telepathic race, it seems unlikely that this deception could go on for long without being detected."

"As you well know, telepathy can be blocked," replied Aoléon. "It is also possible that others have been replaced, as well."

"But wait…you mean you already knew these reptiloids could shape-shift?" queried Gilbert.

"In theory, yes. However, few have witnessed it first-hand. The Draconians are a very secretive race — not welcoming to outsiders. It is part of the warrior mentality that is interwoven throughout their culture — a mindset filled with paranoia and fear."

"Some say that they are soulless beings controlled by dark, energetic, non-corporeal entities, or what you Terrans might call a spirit or demon. A small minority are rumored to have somehow usurped the control of these dark beings and have become 'enlightened' Dracs," added Aoléon. "I only mention that so as not to spread a stigma about their species."

"Stigma? Are you kidding?! Aoléon, these overgrown iguanas just tried to eat us alive! Not to mention that they are going to invade my planet. And you're worried about stigmas? Sorry, but I'm with Bizwat on this one."

"Then again, you just met one of their highest rulers, a Ciakar, and lived to tell the tale, which is equally rare," said Bizwat. "Few, if any, can claim that."

"And thanks to you, Bizwat, the conversation ended with his head on a platter instead of ours!" Gilbert grimaced, his thoughts drifting to his experience with the Luminess. When I saw the Luminess and fell into a dream, a demon tried to kill me. "Can these reptiloids attack you in your dreams?"

"It is easier for them to attack you when asleep. They leach your life force energy and feed off fear," Aoléon replied.

"So, what does this all mean?"

"What we know is that the Luminon is trying to force Mars into a war with Terra over milk and that the Draconians are secretly behind it. We need to get this information to the right people so that we can try to stop the invasion," said Bizwat.

"We will have to be very cautious about to whom we pass on this information," added Aoléon. "If the Luminon is one of them, anyone in our government or the military could be compromised."

Bizwat nodded in agreement.

"What about that Pax guy? He was the one who told you about the Luminon and the invasion in the first place. Remember?"

"I will try to communicate with Pax," said Bizwat. "You two should keep a low profile. You do not want to attract any unwanted attention to yourselves. There could be very harsh repercussions."

Aoléon and Gilbert nodded. Just as Bizwat finished, Pax's form appeared before them on the holokron.

"Deus ex machina!" cried Aoléon.

"Greetings, Pax," said Bizwat. "We were just talking about you."

"Congratulations on discovering and destroying the secret Draconian base hidden inside the Phobos moon. As you have now seen for yourselves first-hand, the Draconians are secretly behind the invasion of Terra."

"Why did you not tell us this before?" inquired Aoléon.

"You would never have believed me. Now listen carefully. You three must seek out the Desert Kýrios. He will then guide you to the secret underground base where the Martian invasion force is being built. I will await you there. Go now. Do not wait."

"But what underground base? Where do we find this Kýrios?" asked Aoléon. But before she could finish her sentence, the connection was severed. Pax's holographic image disappeared.

Aoléon turned to Gilbert and spoke to him privately. "If you would like, we could take you home," she said softly. "I never meant to put you in danger."

"Aoléon, it's really not your fault. You saw what happened back there. The reptiloids are going to invade Earth — my home! My parents, my friends, and everyone I care about are going to be wiped out. So, I can't leave. It's just like Pax told us — that it's now our job to stop them. Only we can do this — us…together."

Aoléon nodded silently.

Gilbert spent the remainder of the trip staring through the transparent hull of the saucer, pondering what they had seen, the incredible things they had survived, and the circumstances that had brought them together in this alien world.

The setting sun sparkled off the enormous domes of the Martian megalopolis — dazzling rays of gold and orange danced like fireflies caught in a red flame. The Intergalactic Spaceport glowed a metallic blue and orange as they flew toward the landing bay. The giant portal to the spaceport opened, and Bizwat piloted the ship into the hangar, setting it down on the designated landing platform alongside hundreds of other ships. Gilbert and Aoléon thanked Bizwat once more for coming to their rescue, said their goodbyes, and phased back to Aoléon's home for the night.

GILBERT
SKYBOARDS
CHAPTER TWELVE

LUMINON'S PALACE
MARTIAN MEGALOPOLIS
OLYMPUS MONS
PLANET MARS

The Luminon's enormous throne room buzzed with activity. The Luminon spoke to one of the Draconian battalion commanders via the holokron situated in the center of the great throne room. As they discussed the plans for the pending invasion of Earth, the Phobos moon exploded, severing their communications link.

"Bring me Sisyphus!" commanded the Luminon, slamming his fists against the console that surrounded the holokron.

A moment later, Sisyphus, head of Martian Intelligence, entered the room to give a report on the progress of the preinvasion force.

"Report!" commanded the Luminon.

"I am afraid that the main Draconian base on Phobos has been completely destroyed. We lost a quarter of a million troops and equipment — ten divisions, my Luminon."

"How can this be?"

"The investigation is underway as we speak, my Luminon. What little evidence we have collected so far seems to indicate that an extremely powerful antimatter explosive planted deep within the moon base itself destroyed it. It has the hallmarks of a Procyon operation."

"Impossible! The Procyon are under our control! How could it be a Procyon operation?"

"We think the resistance may have the support of a rogue Procyon commando."

"I want you to interrogate everyone in the Procyon chain of command and find out what happened!"

"As you wish, my Luminon."

"What else?" the Luminon snarled.

"We destroyed another one of the Terran's primitive Mars probes. This one was called 'Beagle.' The one our spies in the Terran European Space Agency warned us about."

"It seems that the Terrans have an acute interest in our planet. They are a major threat that must be dealt with immediately."

"As you wish. Fortunately, a small contingent of Draco warriors survived. They departed for Mars prior to the destruction of Phobos and are staging themselves in the underground Martian base in Cydonia as we speak."

"Good. Do you think they will be successful?"

"Yes, my Luminon. After we launch the larger invasion force against Terra, the remaining threat should be quickly squashed," Sisyphus replied with an evil grin.

"They will once again become our slaves!"

"As you have foreseen, my Luminon," Sisyphus said with a curt bow.

"Good. And what progress have our spies on Terra made?"

"They are locating all the major cow pastures and dairy production facilities as we speak."

"What is the status of locating the Martian girl and hu-mon boy?"

"We have an informant aiding us who directed us to their whereabouts. The spy is currently tracking their movements."

"Bring her and the Terran boy to me right away. I will interrogate them personally. Pax and the rest of the resistance must be annihilated!"

"By your command, my Luminon," Sisyphus said, bowing. He turned and left the Luminon's throne room.

☉☉☉

MARTIAN SPACE ACADEMY
MARTIAN MEGALOPOLIS
OLYMPUS MONS
PLANET MARS

After class the next day, Aoléon and Gilbert took off from the Martian Space Academy and headed for the commercial district. The two of them flew on Aoléon's skyboard; Gilbert stood behind her clutching her waist. As they soared around enormous buildings and wove their way through dense Martian air traffic, they didn't notice Charm following them in her shiny new saucer.

"Where are we going?" inquired Gilbert.

"It is a surprise," she said as she angled the skyboard into a dive that headed down into the depths of the megalopolis shopping district. Gilbert's stomach lurched a bit as the negative G-forces from her sudden drop almost made him lose his lunch.

They arrived in front of SkyJammers. Gilbert leapt off the board and looked up to see a large circular building. On top of the building stood a giant holokronic projection of a Martian riding a skyboard. The projection peered down at Gilbert and waved him over, inviting him to enter the shop.

He leaned over and spoke to Aoléon. "Is this your skyboard shop?"

"Yup! SkyJammers, the best skyboard shop on Mars."

"So what are we doing here?"

"You said you wanted to learn how to skyboard. Today is your lucky day!"

"SWEET!"

Aoléon hopped off her board, stowed it in a rack, and led Gilbert by hand into the shop. Inside SkyJammers were all kinds of gnarly-looking spacesuits and sleek helmets. Skyboards in all sorts of shapes, sizes and colors hung in suspensor fields along the walls. Some had a silvery metallic finish and brightly colored stripes. Some were "old school" — longer and more rounded with a subdued color pattern.

Others were shorter, sleeker, brighter and featured more aggressive color patterns. They moved past the rows of boards toward the back of the store where an older Martian stood over a hover-bench and worked on a board.

Aoléon and Gilbert didn't notice, but Charm also had quietly entered the store. As they stood examining a rack of skyboards, she placed a very small circular object onto Aoléon's back and ducked out of the store before anyone could notice her.

"What is up, Aoléon?" said the Martian as he greeted them. "Did you ding your board again?"

"No, Mu. I just need a rental for my friend, Gilbert. Gilbert, this is Mu-Eri," said Aoléon as she extended her arm toward him. "He is a legend and a pioneer. He designed one of the first skyboards — the Vectrex Aeolus. He practically started the sport single-handedly."

"Hello, Mr. Eri," said Gilbert. "Honored to meet you, sir."

"A Terran, eh? Welcome to Mars…and please call me Mu!" he said with a wave.

"That's quite a collection of boards you've got there, Mr. Mu," said Gilbert as he gazed at the assortment of skyboards lining the walls of the shop.

"You bet your asteroids, kid. This is the best skyboard shop in the galaxy!" he said, smiling as he led them over to a wall rack with rental skyboards. "Let us see…you should be good for a Vectrex Omicron III with astroglide rails and new ZimZala gravitational displacement nacelles. That should give you enough boost to launch your Terran bum into orbit," said Mu with a wink. "Just do not crater, 'kay? Cause I would like it back in one piece if you do not mind."

Gilbert grimaced at the thought of falling thousands of feet to his death, and Mu seemed to register his panicked thoughts. "No worries though, mate, you will do just fine. Aoléon is one of the best goofy-footers around — you are lucky to have her. I am sure she will be a good teacher."

"Nice," said Gilbert with mock enthusiasm. His stomach lurched.

"I will even throw in a gravity displacement glove. You will be flying in no time, kid."

"What are the gravity displacement gloves for?"

"In case you have to bail," Aoléon said. "But no worries. Just follow what I do, and you will come back in one piece," she added consolingly. Gilbert didn't look very reassured. After the crazy saucer ride she had given him back on Earth, he didn't exactly trust her judgment.

Aoléon handed Mu credit chits for the rental and headed outside into the bright Martian sunlight. Gilbert had to squint to adjust for the glare. He glanced down at his newly acquired skyboard and examined its sleek features, noticing a subtle hexagonal weave coating its shiny surface.

"Okay, now you power up the board by hitting this button right here," she pointed to a marking on the side of the board. "Then drop it, and it will hover — ready for you to jump on. The board is linked to your thoughts via the neural link inside your helmet. It will automatically go where you want just by thinking. If you have to bail, hit the button on your glove. That will activate the gravity displacement field to slow your descent and protect you from sudden impact. That is about it. Any questions?"

"Umm…no," said Gilbert, tentatively shaking his head.

"Okay. Time to fly…and relax. You will be fine," she smiled reassuringly at him.

Gilbert watched Aoléon hit the button on her board and toss it out in front of her. He copied what she did. Aoléon jumped onto her board, leaned forward, and took off. Gilbert followed. They flew out over the city together.

"Doing great!" Aoléon said. "You are a natural."

"Thanks!" Gilbert said as he wobbled a bit, almost losing his balance. He quickly regained his footing.

"Now we are going to try some banking maneuvers. Hang on and follow me. Remember, look where you want to go."

Aoléon banked and fell into a dive with Gilbert in close pursuit. Flying the board was a lot easier than he had anticipated. The board read his mind, reacting to his thoughts exactly as it should. Aoléon made several slalom turns, and Gilbert followed close behind. He found that skyboarding was a lot like snowboarding, which he had done many times on visits with his friends to Colorado, except that this was much scarier because he was now more than one thousand feet off the ground.

"Whooo-hooo!" Gilbert gleefully shouted as a huge grin spread over his face.

Aoléon looked back at him and smiled, giving him two thumbs up. "Now for something a bit more advanced — aerials. Copy what I do." She banked quickly on her board and shot up in the air, flying a loop-de-loop. Gilbert followed and managed to pull it off.

"You are a natural," Aoléon beamed.

Gilbert smiled brightly, but the smile was quickly replaced by a worried expression. All of a sudden, Gilbert noticed something strange approaching them.

"Uh…Aoléon look over there! What are those things coming toward us?"

"This is most strange," Aoléon said, frowning as moving objects in the distance came into focus. "Oh wait…Paladins! Move!"

They had been found. The paladins quickly gained on them. The disruptor cannons mounted on their hoversleds burped rapid-fire bursts. Blasts of plasma flew past the duo.

Aoléon screamed, almost losing her balance. They barely avoided several shots that came close to hitting their mark.

"We are in serious trouble," Aoléon yelled, beckoning Gilbert to follow. Aoléon dove downward and Gilbert followed close behind. "Hang on!"

The paladins gained on them. Aoléon made sharp slalom turns, and Gilbert followed her as best he could. The shots continued to fly past them.

"I am going to try to lose them in the buildings. Stay close!"

Why are they chasing us? Gilbert wondered.

No time for questions! Move! Aoléon cried out telepathically.

They zigzagged through a maze of buildings. Up, over, and under archways as well as through some of the larger buildings' tunnels. They flew with the paladins in close pursuit. Reversing her direction, Aoléon suddenly braked and headed directly for the paladins. She turned her board sharply sideways and bent her knees, performing a backscratcher. Aoléon slammed the bottom of her board into the middle of the oncoming paladin's chest, knocking him off his hoversled.

The paladin's hoversled exploded into pieces, and he fell, slammed into a building, bounced twice in rag-doll fashion, and then kept falling thousands of feet to the ground below. The other three paladins turned to follow her, and two of them collided in the confusion but quickly recovered. Aoléon turned sharply, and using her psionic power, sent a force-bubble at the second paladin, knocking it sideways off its sled. The second paladin collided with the side of a building and tumbled to the ground. Aoléon turned back toward Gilbert and accelerated, quickly catching up with him. The two remaining paladins regrouped and continued to fire.

Gilbert, we are going to let them catch up to us, and when they do, I want you to hit the little green button on the back of your glove and jump off.

Aoléon and Gilbert slowed a bit, letting the two paladins gain on them. Suddenly Aoléon shouted, "Now!" She aimed her board at the paladins and jumped off mid-flight. Gilbert did the same.

Both skyboards flew right into the two paladin guards, causing an enormous explosion. Gilbert and Aoléon flew through the air. Aoléon somersaulted three times and then extended her arms and legs straight out. Gilbert did the same, his body spinning and his stomach doing loop-the-loops. He barely kept conscious while blood rushed from his head. Gilbert thought he was going to be sick, but there was no time to worry about that as the ground rushed up at him from far below.

"Ahhhh!" screamed Gilbert as he spun through the air.

Activate the gravity displacement button on your glove! shouted Aoléon telepathically to Gilbert as they rapidly descended thousands of feet toward the ground and the city below.

Hit the button! cried Aoléon telepathically as Gilbert continued to fall, arms flailing in the wind. The ground was coming up fast as they flew past several arching ambulatory passageways just barely missing them.

The–button–on–your–glove! cried Aoléon. Gilbert froze. The immensely tall Martian buildings flew past and the ground rushed up to meet him. Images flew through Gilbert's mind — his family, his kitty Xena, his friends, and how his relatively short life was about to come to an abrupt and sticky end.

Use–your–glove! cried Aoléon in desperation. At the last second, Gilbert came out of his shock-induced haze, focused his thoughts, and hit the button on his glove. It cocooned his body in a blue bubble of protective energy. Aoléon did the same just before they both slammed into the ground and bounced several times, finally rolling to a stop in the middle of a crowd of Martians. The force field deactivated, and after a moment, Aoléon stood up slowly. She moved over to Gilbert and gently helped him up.

"We made it!" she gasped.

"Yeah we did!" exclaimed Gilbert, adrenaline still pulsing through his veins from the near-death experience. The euphoria made him giddy with laughter. "You were amazing. I mean, ZOIKERS! How did you do that? You…like… single-handedly took out all those paladin guards."

"It was nothing really. Psi-ball training paid off, I guess. You did amazingly well yourself for a first-timer!"

"Except I destroyed Mu's skyboard. He won't be too happy about that. But I am glad to be alive, for sure." They hugged while the surrounding crowd just stared at them in amazement.

"Time to go home."

"Why do you think they were chasing us?"

"Those were paladins, which means the Luminon has found us. We need to get home quick."

"But how? The skyboards were destroyed."

"We are going to phase. It is the fastest way, really."

"Wait, hold on," Gilbert said, grabbing Aoléon by the shoulder. "There is something stuck to your back." He took the postage-stamp-sized homing beacon from her back and examined it closely. "What do you make of this?"

She examined it closely. "It could be some kind of tracking device. Maybe that is how the paladins found us." Aoléon was perplexed. She took the device, threw it on the ground and stomped on it, crushing it.

"I think we need to be extra careful from now on," Gilbert said. "Someone doesn't like us very much."

"Here, take my arm," Aoléon said as she linked arms with Gilbert. "Hold on tight. Here we go!" With a burst of light, Gilbert was squeezed into nothingness and blacked out. The next thing he knew, they were standing inside Aoléon's house. He took several deep breaths as the tingles left his limbs and he could move once again.

"We made it," Aoléon exhaled.

Gilbert removed his helmet and exhaled deeply. "That was incredible," he said just as Zoot came running out from Aoléon's bedroom and shot out his long tongue, giving Gilbert a big, wet kiss on his forehead. "Yuck!"

Aoléon reached down and gave Zoot a pat on his back. Gilbert looked around and saw that everything had been broken and tossed around as if a tornado had crashed through their living room.

"Look at your stuff!" Gilbert cried. "It's all broken!"

Aoléon scanned the room. "Mother, Father, Una…you here?" Aoléon called out, but there was no answer. "Mother, Father, Una—" She called out again. She heard a crash near her bedroom. They rushed to investigate. As they peered around the corner, they saw Una, Aoléon's sister, climbing out from an overturned crate of clothes.

"Are you hurt?" Aoléon asked as she hugged her sister. Una began to cry. "Everything is okay now. I am here." Una continued to cry, clutching tightly onto Aoléon.

"What happened?" Aoléon held her.

"Bad men came…," Una said, choking with tears. "I hid from them, but I could hear them talking."

"Who?" Aoléon asked softly.

"Paladin guards, I think," Una said, sniffling.

"Where are Mother and Father?"

"I do not know. They took them…I want Mommy," Una began to cry again.

"Do you know where they took them?"

"Something about wanting to ask Mommy a bunch of questions," Una said as she wiped her nose.

"They must have been taken to the Xiocrom," Aoléon told Gilbert. "Una, how about you go stay with grandma while I go find Mother and Father."

"Grandma," Una croaked, tears glistening on her puffy blue cheeks.

"Can you go by yourself?" Aoléon asked.

"Think so. But I want Mommy!" Una said as she started to cry again.

"I know. The most important thing right now is to get you somewhere safe. Go stay with grandma while I go find Mother and Father, understood?" Aoléon said consoling her.

"Affirmative," Una said sniffling, and then the room flashed as Una phase-jumped away. Zoot hopped over to Aoléon and lay his head against her leg.

A flash of light, and Pax appeared in front of them. Aoléon and Gilbert leapt backwards; Zoot let out a "BRRREEET."

"Aoléon, please listen. I come with important news. The Luminon has taken your mother and father to a secret Xiocrom detention area located in an underground base beneath the Great Pyramid of Cydonia. They are now prisoners of the Xiocrom…charged with high treason."

"Why were they arrested?"

"The Luminon is actively searching for you and the Terran boy. In your absence, they captured your parents, suspecting that they, too, were part of the resistance. The megalopolis is no longer safe. You need to escape now while you still can. I will meet you at your final destination after you have arrived at the secret underground base in Cydonia."

"Escape? Where to?" Aoléon asked, half choking.

"As I told you before, you must first seek the desert Kýrios. He will prepare you for your journey." In a flash, Pax vanished from the room.

"He is right. We can't procrastinate any longer. We must do what he says," Gilbert said. "We need to go find this guy."

"I am afraid," Aoléon said, looking up at Gilbert with a forlorn expression.

"Nothing is impossible. And nothing happens by chance. You helped me believe that! I am here for you, and I am not going to leave you," Gilbert said, grasping her arm and leading her toward the door.

"Wait. I need to find Bizwat. He will help us," said Aoléon. She closed her eyes. After a moment, she opened her eyes again and rubbed them with the back of her hand. "He agreed to meet us at the Martian Space Academy."

"Then let's go find him," Gilbert said, taking Aoléon's hand in his own. "Come on. Time to do your phasey-thingy!"

Aoléon tilted her head toward Gilbert and half-smiled; a tear streaked down her cheek. She gently leaned over to him and gave Gilbert a kiss on his cheek. She clutched Gilbert's arm tighter, and in a flash, they disappeared.

Continue the saga in
Part Four: "Illegal Aliens"

GLOSSARY

A.I. — An abbreviation for *artificial intelligence* — a thinking, sentient machine or computer.

A. I. hacking — Breaking into and manipulating artificial intelligence (see **A.I.**) to do your bidding.

AU — An abbreviation for *Astronomical Unit*. An Astronomical Unit is the mean distance between the Earth and the Sun. In 2012, the International Astronomical Union defined the distance to be 149,597,870,700 meters or about 93 million miles.

arcologies — Enormous, raised-pyramid hyperstructures that are self-contained microcities in a single, gargantuan building. They combine high population density residential habitats with self-contained commercial, food, agricultural, waste, energy, and transportation facilities.

Aurora Interceptor — A fictional interceptor version that I created for this book of the U.S. Air Force Aurora spy plane. "Aurora" was the code name for the U.S. Air Force's replacement for the SR-71 spy plane. The Aurora went into service in 1989. It was capable of flying into space without aid of rocket boosters, orbiting the Earth, and landing on the ground. It could fly at speeds in excess of Mach 12 within the atmosphere.

bovars — Martian cows that are saurian in origin, hatched from eggs, and produce a milk-like substance used in making galact (see **galact**), the main foodstuff of the Martian people.

Ciakar — A term used for *Draco Prime* — the Draconian (see **Draconian**) ruling caste. A Ciakar can range from 14 feet to 22 feet tall (4.3 meters to 7 meters tall) and can weigh up to 1,800 pounds (816 kg). The most distinguishing features of the Ciakar, the supreme leader of the Draconians, are white scales and large dragon wings — features that the other subcastes of the Draconian race do not possess. This is what distinguishes the Ciakar as royalty among the dragon race. A Ciakar also possesses some psionic power — telepathy and telekinesis; however, it is not nearly as strong as in some of the other alien races.

CQB — An abbreviation for *close quarters battle*. CQB is the art of tactical combat while indoors.

Deimos — See **Phobos and Deimos**.

Draconian — A reptiloid species originating from the constellation Orion. They were the first sentient species in our galaxy to have interstellar space travel (more than four billion years ago). Their society is based on a hierarchical caste system in which the leaders constitute a separate species known as the Ciakar (see **Ciakar**). The castes are royalty, priest, soldier, worker, and outcast.

Draco Prime — See **Ciakar.**

DUMB — An abbreviation for *Deep Underground Military Base.*

EBE — An abbreviation for *Extraterrestrial Biological Entity* — another term for alien.

ESA — An abbreviation for *European Space Agency* (NASA for Europe).

FBI — An abbreviation for *Federal Bureau of Investigation.*

galact — A milk-like substance that is the primary food for the Martian people.

GSG-9 — An abbreviation for *Grenzschutzgruppe 9*. GSG-9 is the elite counter-terrorism and special operations unit of the German Federal Police.

holokron display / holokronic display — A holographic projector and communications device.

Luminess — The spouse of the Luminon.

Luminon — The supreme ruler of Mars.

Majestic Twelve (MJ-12) — A secret committee of scientists, military leaders, and government officials formed in 1947 by an executive order of U.S. President Harry S. Truman to investigate UFO activity in the aftermath of the Roswell crash incident.

MAJIC — See **Majestic Twelve**.

MJ-12 — See **Majestic Twelve**.

nanites — Microscopic robots that perform various enhancement actions.

NASA — An abbreviation for *National Aeronautics and Space Administration*.

NOFORN — An abbreviation for *no foreign nationals*. NOFORN is a designation for classified documents that means that no foreign nationals should be permitted to see them.

NSA — An abbreviation for *National Security Agency*. The three-letter alphabet soup agency is lovingly called "no such agency" by its spook insiders. It is responsible for running the global ECHELON System — a signal intelligence-gathering network that sucks up and records all phone, satellite, Internet, and data worldwide.

NYPD — An abbreviation for *New York Police Department*.

omnitool — A hand-held computer device that can perform a multitude of functions including being able to hack door locks as well as deactivate force fields and turrets.

omniverse — The conceptual ensemble of all possible universes with all possible laws of physics.

ORCON — An abbreviation for *originator controlled*. ORCON is the intelligence marking signaling that material contained is "originator-controlled" and cannot be distributed further without the National Security Agency's permission.

paladins — See **Royal Paladin Elite Guards**.

parsec — A unit of astronomical distance in which 1 parsec = 3.26 light years or about 19 trillion miles, 1 mega-parsec =1 million parsecs or 3.262 million light years, and 1 light year = the distance light travels in one year. Long story short, it is a ludicrous distance to travel so quickly because it is a distance far beyond most people's ability to comprehend.

phase-jump — See **phase-matter jump**.

phase-matter jump — The ability to shift to the post-plasma beam state of matter and teleport yourself and others instantly to another location using only your mind.

phase-shifting — See **phasing**.

phasing — The ability to shift or change matter states. See also **phase-matter jump**.

Phobos and Deimos (moons) — The two moons of Mars that are named after the two horses of the Greek god of war meaning "fear" and "dread." They are roughly the size of large asteroids and have artificially circular orbits around the equator of Mars. The ratio of Phobos's orbital period to Deimos's orbital period is almost clock-like in that Phobos is the minute hand and Deimos the hour hand. Deimos orbits once every 30.4 hours and Phobos every 7 hours 39 minutes.

plasma — The fourth state of matter. A state of matter in which atoms and molecules are so hot that they ionize and break up into their constituent parts: negatively charged electrons and positively charged ions.

Royal Paladin Elite Guards — The select guards of the Luminon.

Schwarzschild radius — The variable radius setting that determines the size of the micro-singularity. The higher the setting, the larger the event horizon and, subsequently, the greater the area of destruction. Dialed down to its lowest setting, it could target a single individual within a crowd while leaving the others unharmed. At its maximum setting, it could destroy an entire planet. Note to operator: using this weapon at its maximum setting is inadvisable.

sentinels — Flying robotic sentries that guard Martian airspace around the megalopolis and conduct reconnaissance for the Xiocrom. Most of the time, the sentinels remain cloaked or invisible.

sentrybot — A security robot designed for basic policing and guard duty. It is less powerful than a soldierbot.

singularity — A singularity is associated with black holes. It is a situation in which matter is forced to be compressed to a point (a space-like singularity).

SITREP — An abbreviation for *situation report.*

Terra / Terrans — Terms that mean *Earth / Earthlings* and refer to the Earth and / or to people who inhabit the Earth.

umbra (classification) — The highest level of classification.

VTOL — An abbreviation for *Vertical Takeoff and Landing.* VTOL refers to an aircraft that is capable of lifting off like a helicopter and then transitioning to regular flight like an airplane.

Xiocrom — The artificial intelligence that controls all Martian governmental functions, the bot and drone workforces, and the robot invasion forces.

Note: Many of the above definitions came from Wikipedia, the free online encyclopedia. I would like to thank their many anonymous authors whose explanations have contributed to the project.

For Xena, who kept me company and made me laugh while I spent countless hours working on this book. For Dad, who helped me when times were tough, and for Mom and Aunt Gwen, who helped edit numerous drafts of this book. And for Jennifer, who inspired me to make the lead character female.

CPSIA information can be obtained at www.ICGtesting.com
Printed in the USA
LVOW05s2241040615

441293LV00035B/776/P